Duck, Duck, Goose!

For Katie — KH
For Roger and Leonie — LR

Note

Once a reader can recognize and identify the forty-eight words used to tell this story, he or she will be able to successfully read the entire book. These forty-eight words are repeated throughout the story, so that young readers will be able to recognize easily the words and understand their meaning.

The forty-eight words used in this book are:

a	chase	fun	it	pass	this
again	come	goose	last	past	try
all	day	high	let's	play	you
and	duck	hooray	like	rest	your
back	fast	I	luck	run	you're
be	faster	I'll	made	so	wind
best	fly	I'm	me	some	with
by	fox	is	on	the	won't

Library of Congress Cataloging-in-Publication Data

Hall, Kirsten.
    Duck, duck, goose! / by Kirsten Hall; illustrated by Laura Rader.
      p. cm. — (My first reader)
    Summary: While running from the "goose" in a game, the boy imagines himself flying through a forest, crossing finishing line first, and being carried by a gust of wind.
    ISBN 0-516-05372-1
    [1. Games — Fiction. 2. Imagination — Fiction.] I. Rader, Laura, ill.
    II. Title. III. Series.
PZ7.H1457Du 1995
[E] — dc20

95-10105
CIP
AC

Duck, Duck, Goose!

Written by Kirsten Hall   *Illustrated by Laura Rader*

CP Children's Press®
A Division of Grolier Publishing
New York London Hong Kong Sydney
Danbury, Connecticut

Text © Nancy Hall, Inc. Illustrations © Laura Rader.
All rights reserved. Published by Children's Press®, Inc.
Printed in the United States of America. Published simultaneously in Canada.
Developed by Nancy Hall, Inc. Electronic page composition by Lindaanne Donohoe Design.
1 2 3 4 5 6 7 8 9 10 R 05 04 03 02 01 00 99 98 97 96 95

Duck,

duck,

duck,

duck,

Goose!

9

You're goose!

I'm on the run!

Run faster, faster, this is fun.

Come chase me, chase me

past the rest.

15

Come chase me, chase me.

Try your best.

I'm like a fox,

I run so fast.

I'm like a fox,

I won't be last.

I'm like the wind,

I'll pass you by.

I'm like the wind,

I fly so high.

I made it back.

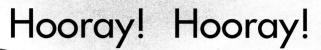

Hooray! Hooray!

Let's play again.
Let's play all day!

Let's play again,
and with some luck,

I won't be Goose.

I'll be a duck!

ABOUT THE AUTHOR

Kirsten Hall was born in New York City. While she was still in high school, she published her first book for children, *Bunny, Bunny*. Since then, she has written and published fifteen other children's books. Currently, Hall attends Connecticut College in new London, Connecticut, where she studies art, French, creative writing, and child development. She is not yet sure what her plans for the future will be—except that they will definitely include continuing to write for children.

ABOUT THE ILLUSTRATOR

Laura Rader was born in New Jersey and raised in Connecticut. She studied fine arts and graphic design at Pratt Institute in Brooklyn, New York, and has illustrated numerous books for children. Recently she moved across the country to Los Angeles, California. Rader especially enjoys listening to her friend Scott play his drums. She also enjoys cartoons, aerobics, music, and her very large "family" of stuffed animals.